ARRANGEMENT

FICTIONS

MERRIDAWN DUCKLER

Also by Merridawn Duckler

Interstate
(Dancing Girl Press)

Idiom
(*Harbor Review*)

Misspent Youth
(Rinky Dink Press)

ARRANGEMENT

FICTIONS

MERRIDAWN DUCKLER

STHRNMST BKS

SAINT AUGUSTINE, FL 2024

For more information:
SouthernmostJournal@gmail.com

Published by Southernmost Books

Saint Augustine, FL

First Edition
ISBN: 9798218448059

Typeface: Abadi Extra Light, Georgia

Cover and interior design: Gavin Stephen Lambert III

Cover illustration: Adobe Stock (Yurii Andreichyn)

Table of Contents

For Bryan

You're an idiot, babe
It's a wonder that you still know how to
breathe

Bob Dylan

Arrangements

There was a Help Wanted sign at the florist's. I had a car, so I walked in and applied. This was a time in my life when I'd decided anyone could do anything. In other words, I was an artist. I had no "experience" but who becomes a professional flower deliverer? Although deconstructing Dutch still life flowers had been an assignment in my MFA from our teacher who looked like a monk and drank like one too.

In that era, there were maps. Even to this day I can refold a map with authority, although I couldn't have predicted how useless a skill set that would become. The shop was large, cold and empty, awaiting Valentine's Day, June weddings and death. In the backroom leaves lay scattered all over the concrete floor like a destructive baby had trawled a garden.

Doris the owner worked at a long metal table back there, between big white plastic tubs of fisted ferns and damp babies' breath. Doris was short, tough, with three piercings in one ear and none in the other. Her head was outsized, like a warthog's, under a bandy-legged sailor's body. She near slapped the Teleflora sanctioned bouquets into shape, loudly addressing the silent, tall, sandy-haired man next to her covering Styrofoam orbs in gold spray paint. That was her husband. He was like a sous chef for flowers. She always made the same joke, that I should be the one to spray the orbs since I was an artist. She found that a most hilarious profession.

Everyone smoked while they listened to barely audible top forty and expertly jabbed stems into the pin, frog or foam. They'd put a card in the forked pick, ribbon up the cellophane nice and tight, and load everything into the back of my Dodge. One day there was an identical Doris waiting outside the shop when I arrived. Also smoking. Also wearing a stained sweatshirt with the arms cut off.

She left and I stood there as Doris attached a huge funeral spray to a wooden stand that looked like an easel. "My sister," she said, by way of explanation. She stood with her hands on her hips, checking the symmetry of the carnations that formed a cross. "You know what she was, right?" She put down her cigarette and slicked her finger over a drooping rose. "Anyone can tell, right?" Her husband worked silently. "A nun! What a cliché. And now she quit and what the hell is she qualified for now?"

They let me go a few weeks later so I guess that was the answer. Odd jobs. That's the old term for them. And yet the memory comes back so powerfully, barreling down the highway, smoke clinging to my hair, surrounded by flowers, as if I was traveling everywhere in a field that moved.

Lifetime Collection

This Bible came over on the Oregon Trail. I just sold it to a guy in a military mesh-back for three dollars. To my left is the booth of a couple who repaint terrible furniture. To my right is a kid selling off his old toys at this swap meet. I keep mis-reading the sign as Swamp Meet.

Amos is asleep in the truck. He gave me a bag of change, a mug of coffee and a wooden Japanese doll his dad brought back from a mission to Nagasaki. Now the old man is in memory care and we're tasked with selling his stuff.

"If you feel uneasy, look at her."

I went off medication in April. I find it hard to sleep. Takes me six herbs, seven tales, eight breaths, to get even sluggish.

Two women come by. "How much for the hunting hat?"

"Two bucks." They move on. My plan is to go up in price with each failed transaction.

Kid with the toys is a gifted salesman. "Look," he says to each passerby, "the day is winding down so I'm ready to deal." It's 10 a.m.

More people. "Wow, that's a lot of tape. How much for that tape?"

"Fifteen." Might fetch several hundred new. But it's been a while since I was able to shop in a store. Amos does all that. "I'd be dead if not for you," I say conversationally. He wraps me in his coat, two escapees who remain on the grounds of the asylum.

His dad resides in care with his third or fourth wife (mix-up in the seventies). No memory left, especially of all the horrible things he did. If you are a devil in your own country, they may regard you as an angel in another. A girl comes by and stops, baby strapped to her chest. "I have two more at home and these are my step-kids." I took her to be around sixteen. Her child touches the Japanese doll.

"Sorry, not for sale. Family heirloom." The doll's hands hang in soldier's stance, palms to thighs, shape of a clothespin.

I look at the table. How did he accumulate all this shit? And still was able to bring about Amos. A sinner can father a saint. That's the thing about saints. Why maybe you never hear about their parents.

"How much for the box of tape? I could use that at Christmas."

"Twenty."

She buys it. Kid gives me a thumbs up and I'm suddenly aware that others may be assessing my success and failure. A woman in the booth across, selling expensive herbs found free in dirt, comes over to talk to the furniture people. She nods her head vigorously and learns they are retired, inspired and a team. The wind blows the flies away from the lemonade guy. I think about putting up a sign: All is Free. But would this look like a diss on the whole system?

Amos comes up, his hair a feathery mess.

"I'll get food. What do you recommend?"

"Just make it edible." No sainthood without tribulation.

The day trudges on, unimaginably long. The furniture people have sold everything except a blistered mirror. They are bored, on their phones. I try to imagine their life but I really think that's a bad idea. Kid comes over.

"I finished my summer book, got any for me to buy?"

I sold the Bible. Only my books are left, a box containing self-help and the poems of Li Po, another saint who rose to the top of the court and fell from mountains. A devoted husband. I open the bent pages.

"Until only the Mountain remains," I read aloud.

"What? What does that mean?"

"I dunno." The remains of the mountain of crap we have accumulated. The remains of the tiny flame alive in those we used up and abandoned and also loved.

I hold it out. "Here. Isn't it your birthday today?" Kid shakes his head no; he's amused, but unafraid of me.

"Well, now it is. Happy Birthday." We are born every minute, and this is where all our gifts come from in the end.

A Care in the World

I don't care that I got into Big Ivy with a full ride, or State with a Merit. I don't care that grandpa came here with nothing but made something of himself by avoiding low company or that gramma was Gamma Beta or that mom runs a clinic or that dad fixes the world. I don't care that bro is a lawyer and sis is a doctor. I don't care that I was born to go as wide as dreams could take me with my IQ and my tech savvy and my waist and my eyelashes. I don't care that I'm graduating at seventeen because I skipped a grade or that the age of consent is eighteen here but it's sixteen or lower wherever we can drive to in Jeff's Mazda pickup with the bashed in passenger door. I don't care that Jeff likes to show off where his nipple almost got blown off when they kicked him out of the Army after he'd had a few. I don't care what he means by a few. I don't care that I must wipe off the bottle top because it's hilarious to drunk up the hogs. I don't care how mean hogs are, or how the road that leads to his "farm" is a rutted deathtrap. I don't care that the only other National Scholar All-star David Mitaski was so desperate after I dropped him that he actually called mom to find out why. I don't care to relate her response. I don't care that I used to find David Mitaski cute and smart and someone very knowledgeable about Bay Area 70's punk. I don't care that everyone in AP Physics wonders what happened to me. I don't care that the school shrink messaged me how we should talk and how was I doing. I don't care to discuss life goals with a grown man who wears a bow tie. I don't care that Jeff watches me from the plaid couch he accidentally made into two chairs with a chain saw and says baby girl when you stop walking around with a stick up your ass and we get hitched gonna buy you a Beemer like that guy in the movie. I don't care to know what movie he is referencing. I don't care that I have no interest in a car driven by German butchers. I don't care that when Jeff laughs sometimes one of his teeth falls out. I don't care that I am a virgin unlike so many of my so-called friends. I don't care that real men spit and fart and can hold a girl so tight a woman starts to come out. I don't care that crew needs me and can't get to finals now that I won't go to practice. I don't care how on a beautiful day on the lake I got in that accident and went down to the bottom and saw that we are a hair's breadth from death. I don't care that I came out of the hospital just fine, with no detectable injury. I don't care that I sat in the parking lot of Burger King crying and Jeff made me roll down the window and said who just needs to smoke a bowl. I don't care that I don't smoke anything. I don't care that in selfies Jeff looks like someone from the ancient past who was not a gladiator but something they fed to the lions. I don't care that Jeff came to my family party with a penis bouquet but was too drunk to count out the correct number of balls. I don't care how after that mom sat by the Cuisinart and cried and dad sat by our labradoodle and cried and I had never seen dad cry before and I was kinda freaked out. I don't care what has happened to me that I won't go down to the pool anymore, or the tennis court, or how my heart is like that little ball dad taught me to kick when I was seven which was ten years ago and I was so good at that game. I don't care that I can never remember it had the name hacky-sack. I don't care that I don't know what I'm doing or how it will end. I don't care that I sit on my bed, in my bedroom where mom always kissed me goodnight and dad made up crazy shadows on my wall when I couldn't sleep and bro told me he was gay and I held his hand for some reason and sis told me she barfed the last slice and blamed me and was a bad person and I gave her my gold key choker she'd been eyeing while Jeff sits down the road in the Mazda that can't stop won't stop primarily because the engine hasn't been serviced since the early aughts and holds the ring that turned my finger green and waits as I sit and see how moonlight really is kind of beautiful and send some confused thanks to Ms. Markham for having us read the poem by Li Po about wanting the moon and how we will always stagger around alone and how we care anyway and how we care.

Ringling

In the spider-ridden basement, on the stick-legged television, I remember watching the greatest show which was the "The Greatest Show on Earth" with Betty Hutton, basically sex on a straw, purring: "He said I was like champagne, I made his head spin!" She was cast after she sent Cecil B. DeMille a $10K floral arrangement of herself swinging on a branch. Worth every penny! Although Charlton Heston got his role by simply waving a howdy across the Universal parking lot. In fact, they wanted Burt or Kirk or any of those hunks but were stuck with Cornel Wilde's contract instead. Afraid of heights it took him a dozen takes to kiss his hottie upside down on the trapeze, although I managed in a single try (one eye closed) even as my other eye filled with emotion over the scorn of men for carnies, not one of them able to guess why Buttons couldn't take off his make-up. Townies! They're *idiots*! The credits run but I can't move, because that basement is vanished, that television is dead, that spider an ossified thought of a thread unrolled from when I was eight years old and felt

my life was a circus I could only catch a glimpse of as it rolled away to the next small town.

Shipping the Gods of Sitcom

I knew them better than my own family. The mother unlike any mother I'd ever experienced. Her beautiful arm clears the marble counter. Hestia. The piggish brother squeaks from his neat and orderly room. Someone has returned him to human form. Circe. He was Castor and Pollux, for they like to cast twins. The youngest, carried about, emits ignored warnings, a baby repository of folk reason. Cassandra in cribs. Several dangerous sisters, arrayed like marble on stairs and couches. Tightening their hair ties. String. The fates, the fatales. Everyone coming into the room, sprung from the forehead, fully groomed. Fathers in formation with temporary allies: one neighbor, one friend, one co-worker. At night the screen is the width of my oversized torso. My face pixilates into Medusa. Stuffing six kernels of corn into my mouth I wonder what they will have wrought for me this time. The last words of the oracle: No Talking Spring. Maybe missing a comma. No talking, spring. All my life I've wanted an altar. And a laugh track.

Triptych

1.

Fresh paint on every wall of the gallery, except the one where my big piece is going. Why? Biggest wall takes the longest to dry. Makes no sense.

2.

Ward arrived and stood out on the sidewalk. Smokes this candy-flavored stuff now. I said that does a number on my sinuses. He said, Peter, be happy something on you is enflamed. We laid out a couple of paintings, all torsos. Kind of an odd orange patch in one corner.

3.

He said, how are you, you ancient motherfucker? I said I'm fine. No complaints. No complaining means you're dead, he said. I had the #47 against a wall. He said, what's the ratio this time? I said 1:3. He nodded. Nice.

4.

L'anne came to my studio. She was wearing some kind of tent. She said fashion, Pete, ever heard of it? Can you imagine when they feature you in one of those magazine spreads? Have Dinah at least buy you a pair of jeans. I said nice to see you too. She said the Foundation is buying stuff again. You'll show with Ward. He has these torsos. You'll love them. He has a new boyfriend. Let me in. I'm freezing.

5.

I like them. I do not *love* things. I reserve that emotion for people. The long titles are ridiculous. I'm not crazy about my frames. They need to be a half-inch thinner. Dinah agrees.

6.

Ward was up on a ladder. He said, how much of the cadmium can you detect from down there? Held the ladder as he came down. We sat together. He said, Jesus, these couches are uncomfortable. I said L'anne doesn't believe furniture should comfort people. Buyers from the Foundation are hunkered down? That's the scuttle. He said, we're moving to Barcelona right after. He's crazy about Spain. We looked at big wall. He said, it's vaguely massive but not as big as the old ones. I said I can't always get up what I used to. What do you think of the frame? Tactful silence.

7.

L'anne said Ward isn't painting in there is he. He'll fall off that ladder and break his neck. I am not paying his hospital bill. I am not made of money. You do it once and you're beholden forever.

26

8.

The minute the stuff from Ward's flask hit my throat I coughed all over my white shirt. I said, I thought wine. Ward said who on bloody earth puts wine in a flask? Here, use this. I said, you carry a handkerchief? I wasn't raised by wolves. Wipe.

9.

From when I was sick, and it wasn't nice to be spitting up everywhere. The least you can do is not use paper. Like some walking dispenser.

10.

Ward dabbed at my shirt. Did L'anne ask if I was painting on the ladder? Tactical silence. That girl is a piece of work. Still, the best dealer I've had so far. Takes a commission of maybe thirty percent less bullshit. He said, what did you think of the article? I said such a stupid story by that moronic critic. Clout hound. I don't work by accident. Don't shake a brush and get wherever. It was based on the triptych.

11.

The direction of the splatter. Three discrete areas. It's a triptych.

12.

Ward said, the Merode.

13.

Yes, the Merode! You know they'd paint a middle one. To entice a buyer. Something popular. An Annunciation. Good subject for a painting because you spend half your time sitting around, waiting for someone to come and tell you you're anointed.

14.

Ward said for me, Mantegna's Dead Christ. Dead, but not dead. The way it starts at the feet and goes upward. In the clinic I'd sketch and look at the different lamentations. Obsessed, I suppose. I asked him was this our first time or maybe we'd shown together in the seventies in Berlin? I had a sudden memory. He was extremely handsome then. It was ridiculous to look like that.

15.

I said, where are those titles going to fit. Ward said I can't read. I mean, I can but I'm dyslexic. In school I'd focus on the spaces between. I'd read those.

16.

I said the things about Dutch medieval is that the details in those paintings is just phenomenal. It's not a picture, it's a library. Whole world in a lot of little worlds. Just anything after Brunelleschi makes me nauseous. He said, sorry that my hyperrealism offends you. If it helps, they aren't done from life. Or not my life, anyway.

17.

L'anne hid the ladder. Ward lay on the floor. He said you look like shit. I said thanks, nice to see you too. He said, you ever online? I said, for my students, sure. But you have no platform. I said what's a platform. Ward said, are you shitting me, maestro? Such a smart career move, that recluse thing. I should have done that. I should have stopped going to those stupid parties a thousand years ago.

18.

We went outside. We looked in the window. Ward said, it's like your splatters are shooting my torsos. Couldn't believe how good it looked. Some people stopped and stared. I said, L'anne knows what's what. Ward said, what am I going to do about that orange patch? Jesus, I said. The light behind the building bounced. Those triptychs were made for cities. They were essentially urban. A form made for travel. Prescient. Part of their genius.

19.

From the outside, the gallery sounded like an aviary. Dinah wore the necklace I bought her. A small fortune. A small apology for what had happened to me. I said go on ahead. I imagined everyone naked. It was horrible. There's an alley between the buildings. Ward was there in some outfit. I took out a real cigarette and the air was pungent with the past. I said the thing about those triptychs is that the middle is for a buyer and the one before seals the deal, but the last one is strictly for us.

He said a lamentation is meant to stop the gaze. You can't get past the cock but you have to. I said indecision is where the painting gets made. He said who are you quoting? I said me. I thought about the two of us, moving the squares around and around. Days where we just looked. I wanted to say something about love but instead I said the Foundation bought the show. He said I know that. He said, we're having a big success in there, darling. I said yeah, it's the pinnacle of success.

After the Flood

I'm Debbie and this my sister Micky. Micky says we should change our names to something more glamorous. I said, how abouts remnants and shards? Micky said that sounds like a bad female buddy movie where their personalities are that one is tall and one is short. The thing is, I am tall and she is short. We look nothing alike and not much like our mother whose memory fades a little more each day.

Unfortunately, we do look like the old man. His hands, his eyes. There he sits, weeping and wailing over the state of the world. Kind of insulting since we are the state of the world, us Remnant and Shard.

Micky gives me a look. Deb, stop with the stupid names already. I can't really afford to piss her off since we're the only two left. She thinks we should look for others. I think we should experiment and make life ourselves. She says we should be building stuff with the animals who haven't run off. But it's hard. We do nothing. It's difficult to care when there's no future in sight.

We lie under the blankets that came with the elephants. Mickey remembers the creak of the oars. I remember the obsidian-eyed raven. We never talk about what happened to Mom. We never talk about our old city. It just gets us into a crying jag and then we really do resemble the old man. Micky suggested one time we go and check on him. Absolutely no way, I replied. He's part of the problem and you know it.

What fills our heads is this question. Why us? We weren't the smartest or the best. I might be the prettiest but that's only if you like tall girls. Mickey asks it over and over: why did we make it out and everyone else is gone?

There's no reason I say, rolling over, pinning the edge of the blanket. She's always hogging it in the middle of the night and I end up completely exposed. The blanket does stink, but why should I have to be cold.

In the morning we lay flat in the sun. Micky made us sunglasses out of skin the snakes shed. She's clever. But I'm the one who can cook. I said, look maybe it's just meant that we grow old together, all alone on earth.

Yeah, says M, but what about the continuation?

We'll be the continuation.

Yeah, but we're all eventually gonna die.

Then we glance over at the old man and it's clear whose gonna die first. Lately I've been leaving him a plate of wild yams. It means nothing, we never speak. But hasn't he been through enough without starving?

He really does have our same eye color.

What time is it, asked M. When she wakes up she looks like a sock monkey. I glanced in the piece of metal we use as a mirror. My hair's a mess, I don't even bother combing it anymore. Mickey searched for her old purse.

Look, she said, this is stupid. We're gonna pull ourselves together and go look for some more people. Preferably boys.

She did my nails and I did hers. I put on my only dress. I think I've grown since we got here. It was shorter. Mickey put on a robe, I know it was an old one of Mom's. We heard the whispers start up again. We hear them sometimes. I never talk about it because it does make us seem insane.

I'm getting kind of sick of wild yams, I say, how about we go look for some other food? Mickey stands. I know she hears the voices too, like wind, except with words. We just don't discuss it. We follow the voices when they come. We go up the hill when they say go up and down the path when they say go down the path. We stop when they say stop and this time there was a cave. It wasn't there yesterday.

We overlooked this.

No, it wasn't there before.

The air blows warm at the entrance. The voices become insistent. I can see in Mickey's eyes that she is afraid. I put my arms around her. I'm the older, after all. We step in together. My toe hits something. It's a bottle of wine. There are two bottles of wine. One for her to use and one for me. The voices roar. An image of Auntie Eve comes into my mind. What do we really know about why we are here after all. History starts with that question.

Window on the World

There were four of us. Girls often traveled in fours at that time, like free restaurant crayons. Really three and we rotated the fourth. We played cards where we hid from adulthood, in a bathroom in the unpopular part of our suburban high school. The card game was one we had made up called Chinook. We named it after a bar we planned to go to, in six years, the Chinook, a depressed, colonial brick-front bar, with neon lottery signs and red vinyl booths for career alcoholics to seat their girlfriends. We'd lift Sunny up to the window and have her report back what she saw. This was after school was out, three or four in the afternoon, in the tiny, meaningless downtown. Rent was cheap then. Thrift shops on consecutive blocks served shady non-profits. Push the non-electric doors open and there was that thrift store scent: permanent markers and shame. I'd go into them, buy some old plate or rumpled poster, thinking how in years and years it would be worth something because everything that was worth something was far older than me.

Carly was overweight. She didn't give a shit. It was youthful weight, and plenty of boys looked into it. Sun was adopted. Korean, with two pale white parents, discussing whether or not to put a pool into the backyard or where it would even go. Her Mom smoked Virginia Slims. We wished she had better taste, since that meant we too had to smoke Virginia Slims, but we were accepting of our fate. Sun had older brothers, also adopted. No one in the family looked anything like each other, even her parents were mismatched. Sun was thin, her hair long. Her face was damning in its beauty. She had no boyfriend. Boys were afraid of a girl that perfect. It wasn't a time of bravery among boys. Everyone was keeping quiet, so as not to attract the attention of another war.

We played cards in the bathroom and smoked. No teachers came in, except on arranged busts, like in Casablanca. We were model prisoners, lifers who had forgotten the sentence, the existence of a release date. Others, day trippers, played hearts or fuck your buddy. Only we understood Chinook. No one could use the toilets, in fact they were damaged, vandalized, most of the doors didn't close. If you couldn't hold it and had to shit, we'd wave three-ring binders disconsolately until it passed. Even as our language was filthy our outlook was conservative. I told Sun she would be a great lawyer someday. For that she pulled a knife on me, but it was a butter knife. We often acquired things that could potentially be turned into weapons if we weren't so lazy and uneducated.

Sun would let us lift her up to look in. She was strong, but almost weightless. Mine was the back she stood on, looking in windows of the bars that were usually closed until at least four, the hour before all tragedy commences. She would describe the interior in detail, the number of booths, state of holes in the dart board. Lettering on the jukebox. Her descriptions were vivid as dreams, and also faded by the following day. No one really stopped us, walking around the several daytime restaurants struggling to stay in business for smart-dressed lawyers hurrying into the courthouse while the dejected criminals sat outside on benches in the yellow light. No one cared about us, loitering beside banks with cement rolls on top, Corinth columns that once meant temples. If we saw a cop turning the corner we ran. Once one did stop, we decided not to run. Where would we go? Most places didn't open until six. The officer got out of the car. He was the age we'd be when our age doubled. He turned to Carly first and asked her name. She said Carly Marly. He said don't flip me that shit, sister and then his dashboard lit up with a real crime and he roared away. Carly had gotten us off a sure ticket by saying her real name, which was in fact Carly Marly. Her parents' drunken joke had finally paid off. We didn't tell the story to anyone right away. There wasn't so much value in us that we could afford to throw around a good story like that to just anyone.

We'd often walk around with the fourth person who was rotational. We'd take her to parts of the city we knew, secret ones, lesser known fountains you could stand in. We wore bikini tops over jeans. Men would shout at us but we never answered. Walking along, smooth as a birch, in black boots, our smooth long neck, chins shaped like the pockets on pool tables. If we could only stand beside them we'd be as cool as a boy.

One of these fourths was Margot. Another was Susan, thin and warmth-colored like Sun but with poor posture and hair that didn't go anywhere. Sometimes a more popular girl would come, almost on a dare or as some kind of initiation. We realized in some universe we were considered tough and dangerous but it might be years before anyone confirmed it. Carly had a box cutter. She trimmed her nails with it when we were dealing Chinook, but it made her cuticles bleed and the blood fell on the floor of the bathroom, reminding us of our notoriously copious periods when we would cry, for many reasons. Others in the bathroom, fixing a face, just let that slide. Just another girl, crying.

Game Theory

Becky is a bully. Her sister, Corey, should have been a boy. These are facts which Corey knows to be as certain as the word *facts*, fat middle letters fenced in by two taller guard letters. Becky makes her crouch in Spiderville, under the cinderblock foundation and stay there until Becky says she can come out. Once Corey had to stay until dinner, and she got in trouble. But she never ratted out Becky and the look Becky gave her over tomato barf casserole was a look to hold at night when a person is too old for dolls.

Becky can bully colors. When that man asked them their favorite color and Becky said "Purple," Corey could not see any other color. Purple ruled the universe. "Go outside and play," said their mother. The man smiled down at them as they ran off. Now he makes a funny face out the window. Corey knows for a fact this face is for Becky. Becky ignores the men in cars whistling through their teeth, making a rolling motion to take down the window, while Mom stands in the grocery, reading ingredient lists. In the park in summer Becky will agree to take free ice cream and money, but she never looks back and smiles only to herself as she tosses away the cone.

Corey is glad they've been sent into the yard to play. It's spring. The flowers are crazy. The sun is coming over the fence like the word *feckless*. Becky wears no jacket. She has on the madras shirt Mom bought her that leaves skin between her jeans and boobs. When Mom came in that night to tuck in Corey, "There's a lot in you to love," she whispered, sitting next to her in the bottom bunk, making it hard to breathe through the beauty. "Never forget that, Coraline, sweetheart, baby girl." Corey wishes she was a boy right that moment and then Mom could have what she wants: a girl, Becky and a boy, Corey.

Now that they're outside they don't know what to do. Becky throws pinecones at Spiderville. Corey jumps on and off the big log separating their house from the doublewide. She starts to follow Becky around, and Becky pushes her away. Corey says "No, no, no, no." It's an invitation to play the game they made up. It has no name. Corey calls it "No Game."

In this game a person chases a person, but that person can stop them by saying "No." After they say that, the other person can move two times to try and tag them. If they are too far away, they can't hear the No. If they are too close, they'll lose. Corey is better at the game, but Becky is better at cheating at the game.

They play No Game in the backyard. They play near the rusted car they are forbidden to touch but they have. Becky screams and runs into the front yard. Her scream is beautiful and shakes the spring sun. Corey would love to scream like that. They stand in the front yard where Corey has Becky at the exact right distance. She has one No left and is deciding how to use it. Becky eyes her with one part. The other is looking at the man at the window. Mother left the room and he is standing, watching them. He taps the glass. "No," says Corey. Becky starts to gallop like a horse around the yard. She gallops in ever tightening circles, then adds a head toss. Only Becky would think of that, her hair flying in the spring air, the pucker of her shirt crawling up, the frayed top of her jeans riding down.

Dream Job

Once I had a job writing blurbs for dreams. I worked out of an office in the old Time/Life building, second floor. Underneath was a trainyard, though few used that kind of transportation anymore. The trains wailed on their way out of the station as I laboriously poked at my computer's many missing keys. I can hear, but only badly mimic that mournful cry. All the ticket offices were either closed or not real windows, instead made from bed frames and fire escapes. Over my desk a fan rotated, creating irritating shadows I'd try and brush away, as if they were cobwebs. The city displayed out the office window was like my town but also not like it, some city from a childhood board game since we like to give children the illusion they build their own home.

My parking spot was up a steep lot, and I often went in the out exit, causing others to honk and yell. If I had to leave for an appointment, all manner of obstacles sprang in my path. In one direction streets were torn up, alleys abruptly went blind. Sometimes I'd end up trying to steer a broken trike while an angry or annoying or simply there-for-the-ride companion who I barely knew or cared about, would comment and judge. Important people showed up en route, people I wished to impress or find a solution to, even members of my own family but they seemed not to hear me, although I'd always find myself running after them, sidelining penguins and umbrellas along the way.

My clientele skewed older, although occasionally a teenager would burst in with a powerful request. They seemed to feel their age made it more important. If they knew what kind of things the adults came up with, they'd blush. It was tense work since the client had the right and even the necessity to tell me the whole dream, often in excruciating detail, but then go back over it for all the parts they forgot. Descriptions defied their limited vocabulary. They tried to explain matters using various metaphors, often with mixed results. They'd shake their heads over disturbing elements that emerged quietly, like a long-ago childhood companion dragging a stuffed animal. Those animals can bite, too. In the dark corridors where no one wanted to go, the oft-times naked client urged me to open doors and walk down streets. I didn't want to do either of those things. But I needed the work.

I tried to get them to see the beauty in even the most outlandish dreams but I wasn't the author, I just wrote the blurb. I'd lay down on my couch, since prone was how I worked best. I knew from experience even if I'd recorded all of our sessions or taken excellent notes, the dream would begin to fade, dissolving into smaller, fainter and more transformed elements, like ash disappearing into the sky from a passionate fire. I'd write "startling" or "important" or "it voices what we all wish we could but can't." Sometimes my pen turned into a stalk of celery or a snake. Without a doubt, this process was frustratingly antiquated. Still, as I unlocked the door to my office, or an office similar to mine but with different furnishings, a long line would have materialized, extending all the way down, as far as the eye could see. People stood, waiting patiently, a tale in their hands burning for a comment from someone other than themselves.

The Aggro

Picture me, hurdling down the sidewalk, game face on, bearing down. Not anyone you'd want to mess with. My pal Jimmy perfected it, some might even say invented it. He's got a massive leg length difference, so he had that going for him. And the drinking. I named it though: Aggro-walking. A sport that lunges straight into the crowd. Akin to a moving mosh pit. Like all athletic endeavors it creates a feeling of pure adrenaline. Major rush. Most find it addictive, myself included. My specialty is doing it in bad weather. Rainy day aggro-er, dodging around the umbrellas, stamping the dirty puddles. Jimmy's more of a fair weather type. Crowds on a bright day. Kids messing with him, won't get out of his path. He says want to take this outside? Extra points if you can cause a moment of self-reflection. Aggro-ed right through them, they couldn't even land a kick. Expected him to run but that's strictly against the rules. Strictly a walking sport. Feet must touch earth at all times. But if you stay tough, they will respect you. I've mowed down some of my best pals now. Measure of a person, actually. The playing field can be anywhere. And how about the time we were in fields, no one for miles. Nothing to pass, nothing to jostle. The trees stood without quarter. No matter how fast you go, it's as if you get nowhere at all. We fell, our eyes upward. Now very clear rules. Can only be in cities. It's a game, after what's said and done. Otherwise, how do you even know you exist? Audience is all.

Loci

Everybody knew the site. It was so common it did not have a name. Children threw rocks into it (I did as a child) and young people made their way up there illicitly. Reigning powers, present then, have become stricter today. But I value such restrictions, they have kept what I seek hidden from the world. Nothing grows for fifty surrounding miles. We traveled by jeep unchallenged. There is one road in and out. The site itself is on a rise, an elevation that either saved or doomed it, it is really impossible to tell.

The guides which accompanied us were hungover from a night of drinking a spirit that was once reserved only for tribal chiefs. It's a vinegary glop compressed in earthen vases and usually sealed with animal fat or the skin of tiny lizards, once abundant here. People said it was vile but irresistible. A hallucinogen. The modern version can be bought in any local market, but it is only a pale shadow of the ancient recipe. The locals wore a hat made from reeds, we wore modern visors and caps. Otherwise we were indistinguishable because all the modern instruments we'd brought with us had been left in the hotel. Our guides were adamant about that since they were worth many times a man's life. I did have one device hidden on me. What was the point of coming here without it?

We camped in the ruins of a structure that had toppled during whatever was the last war. At night, as the cooking fires burned, I smelled again the spiced scent of the wind I had known as a child. The water has the same metallic tang, the ripples of a gong. But I wasn't here to be nostalgic and I was forever grateful I had been able to leave. The men stomped on the denuded ground, saying they could hear an echo, proving there were structures of great size beneath. I think they were afraid their daily pay would be reduced if we came away disappointed. But I already knew it was there. On the edges of my dreams (I slept uncharacteristically badly) I felt my hands trace the ramparts. In my dream the pieces fell apart and my hands bled blue. When I got up in the star-filled night to urinate, I saw an encampment hidden by a low ravine, common here, and felt the presence of women. A child cried and was silenced. In the morning, though, there was only us.

On makeshift tables, boards lodged between camp vehicles, I unrolled the map I carried, rolled inside a dull, official letter. Small fragments were scattered in minor museums around the world, assembling them into this map had been my life's work. Over my head I felt eyes exchange a look. Someone wetted a lip. What lay beneath us was priceless but can never be sold or traded. Possibly cannot even be moved. But human greed is universal and I folded up the map quickly. Identification is one thing, ownership is another. One is the basis of science and art and the other is the basis of violence, theft and war.

We dug before dawn, before the heat made movement impossible and uncovered a new segment. A child might be small enough to slip into the opening and the idea was presented to me but I said no. There's little sentimentality regarding children in the culture. I know this personally. Still, I refused. On the third day the hired men brought me a guide who was dwarfishly small. He had a persistent cough. The others seemed afraid of him, although he wore colors reserved for married men and those with a higher social status. I was alone in my tent, reading, and they brought him to me, without a translator. He knew enough words to make himself clear—he was willing to go between what I believed were two significant but collapsed monoliths and test the stability of the underground entrance. He wanted an extraordinary fee for this, and a signature that if he didn't return the fee would be paid to his spouses.

I agreed. Our time was very short and even though we'd made some progress, the rainy season was coming. That day I was up before dawn. The men claimed it was a religious holiday, possibly they were trying to get more pay. When I came out of my tent I saw they'd pried open a tiny portal. They had wrapped the small man in cloth that was slick with fat and oil. He pointed his toes, which were bare, and with a turning motion, like a bolt, they fit him into the impossibly small opening. It was over in an instant, I hardly had time to take a breath. I think I shouted; I felt the prayer on my parched lips. I touched the device I'd brought in, undetected. Now everything would be revealed, I was thinking when darkness came down on my head.

I awoke in pitch black. The walls echoed like a train station. I got to my hands and knees and shouted, though I knew it was meaningless. My head was pounding. My fingers made circles on the floor until I felt a flashlight and when I turned it on I saw a stack of bottles. The local drink. I could hear a faint crackle of voices above me. Perhaps they were deciding what to do. All of life is a betrayal—did they not think I knew that? I ran the beam up the side of a wall. I was at the entrance itself, the handles were in the unique scallop shape that has never been duplicated before or since. The great doors slid silently apart and I stood up and walked into the hall. Everything from my research was here, eerily, profoundly life-like, the inner circle and balcony, the portico decorated with figures of animals consorting with gods. I heard a command but I couldn't make out the words. I shut off the flashlight and my eyes began to adjust to the dim, sweet air, an improbable source pumping it in. Here is what I had spent the better part of my life seeking. I reached into the hidden pocket of my jacket. The shredder. With a warble it came to life and began to grind the invitation letter they had sent me into tiny pieces of confetti.

The Administrator

We are not sure what J does, but he is exceptionally prompt. On Dough-not Wednesday he arrives early with a tray of celery sticks and ranch. It's a bit of an inside joke because ranch dressing is notably higher in calories than even a dozen doughnuts but as many current and past employees have pointed out, calorie counting is a complex metric. The issue is germane because J himself had begun to grow larger and larger. Our home base has an open office concept, which like most conceptual things—art for example—is almost unbearable in its limitlessness. No walls prevented J from flowing between desks, out into the corridors. Soon he became inadvertently part of every conversation, each meeting began and ended in silence as he wended his way past. Recent hires were mystified. One, without prompting, looked J up in the virtual company roster and saw him listed as THE ADMINISTRATOR, under the (older) picture. The question arose do extra benefits accrue when the presence is greater. The answer apparently is Yes. J is granted sick days into perpetuity, even if he chooses to leave the company. His 401K is still growing. He can't be fired because he is virtually a part of the building. We don't know how J feels about this. His mouth is far off and his eyes are like satellites we mistake for stars. At night, if I'm the last to leave, I shut off the central lights and speak softly since I don't really know where lay his ears. Sorry, man. You are everywhere. Hang in there. Remember the boundless may be a quality of love.

Run

For a marathon you have to train, and train I do. I watch my caloric intake, I do strength and conditioning and run in sun, rain, sleet or snow. I have a team like every dedicated marathoner. My team consists of Road Block Mary, Fuckoff Phil and that guy who goes grr. I used to have Coach Miguel but he died. This affected my soul but not my training schedule.

Training for a marathon is partially mental. I do the numbers. Each lap equals one mile, 26 miles to finish. The track has obstacles, the biggest one being that I live on it. I have no regular house. Coach Miguel said: kid, make that part of your overall. So I do. Garbage under the bridge is good for pull-ups but bad for push-ups. Condemned buildings work for skipping rope but you will often have that rope stolen. Great example: if you need a strict 700 calorie day should you double up at Salvation Army dinner? No way. Far too heavy on carbs.

Fitting in a training schedule is challenging, what with my daily appointments in VA bennies, AA and social services. I usually bring Road Block Mary with me to go see my assigned Angel in social services because I don't like to ride public transport without my invisible cloak and nobody blocks like Mary. She was the team member who got me a lot of newspapers to wear around my chest. I'll tell you though, when I wear that marathon number I will feel as naked as the day I was born.

My Angel in social services is very dedicated to the less fortunate, which includes most of the staff of social services, who are on the lower end of the IQ scale and a bunch of devils to boot. I arrived promptly   as per my usual.

"Mister Charles," said my Angel. "You haven't checked the box that indicates you are taking your meds."

I nodded and took off my hat. It's usually overly hot in the office, which is one way I know we are in hell. Also, where else would need so many angels?

"Angel, I would like to report on everyone, including Phil. I have resolved my issues with the guy who goes grr. Mary is my rock. Miguel, as you know, is dead, although I often hear his voice in my head."

"You hear his voice?" said Angel. She wears a tiny bow in her hair, though I judge her age to be forty plus.

"Not like that," I said. Athletes are often misquoted by a hostile media. Everyone hears the dead's voice in their heads. How else would we speak to them? "Not like that. Not the ones speaking when I remove my cloak of invisibility."

"It's not a cloak, Mister C; it's a pill you need to take for your own safety."

Angel gets fifteen minutes per soul. A medical emergency can stretch that to twenty. I wasn't sure I could accomplish that goal on this particular day, but luck has a surprising history in sports.

"I will take the pills, if we can talk," I said.

She sighed. She looked out the window, displaying a fine and noble profile. I admire her ability to make luxuries of the smallest things.

"OK, then. Tell me about Phil," she said. "But no cursing." Outside her office window I saw those devils had set a fir on fire.

"Phil has been my pacer since day one," I said, "but good runners are tight and light and bouncy, and Phil is a tub of lard. I think his own body issues are getting in the way of my success. Do I owe him loyalty? And what is loyalty? If I ace it, he'll forgive me, as everyone loves a winner, but what if I want to move to ultra?" I sweated through this whole speech because I'd written it out, but Road Block Mary had made me trade it for her grocery list. "Bag of Cheetos," I finished weakly.

We talked it out, just like she promised. I stood and shook her hand. Angels love formality. Modern life has lost so much elegance with these casual Fridays, these dress-like-   roadkill-Tuesdays; it's enough to make us all terrified. As if she could read my mind (and there's every reason to think she can), Angel handed me a little cup of water and a pill.

"It's Christmas," she said. "Do you want something?" She pointed out her office window where I could see a forlorn and naked ham being chased by several of the larger women.

"I'd like to use your calculator," I said. She left and came back with one that must've been made for blind people. It was enormous, the size of a chocolate bar. "From the store room," she said.

I grabbed the calculator and went to work. The guy who goes grr times my laps but what is my overall? Coach Miguel warned me about that. "You're gonna get so wrapped up in the finish, you'll lose sight," he said. "But know this: you won't be judged by the many seemingly huge ways you have totally screwed up your life." I meant to ask him: how will I be judged? But he died before I could. Still, I made some calculations that suggested a plan for the overall. I am so glad I do not have to fire Phil.

I gave the calculator back to Angel. "Would you like to keep it?" she said. Like I really need to walk around with an enormous calculator that will make me look like a total nerd! But it was Christmas and my Angel had done so much for me. "OK," I said, "Merry Christmas." Great example of the power of the marathon training! It is not self-centered, as some suppose, but a symbol of how we move within a great multitude, all with the same goals and yet all totally alone.

Rate My Professor

Is she hard? Like a marble? Rolls around, refusing to pick a side. More a softie? Soft cone? Hard with a soft center? Type to assign seats? Hers or ours? Maybe scramble in the beginning and then everyone stakes their claim. How big are the lectures? Microphone? Megaphone? Run like small, independent nation-states? Popular? Size of a home game? Size of a family holiday no one wants to attend? Does she command a room? Hands move like this? More like a traffic cop? Her eyes: how often do they narrow. All on one side like a flounder? Or jump from face to face. Can she silence with a look? How many? Are we expected to buckle? Down? Is she considered a pushover? Does she push back? Is she like my mother? Is anyone like my mother? How about that sign that says: your mother doesn't work here. Would she laugh at that? Do her classes fill quickly? With tears? Are there escapees. Have they formed a support group? How often do they meet in Room 201? If you wander into class and there she stands—tall-ish but shorter later, mannerly, courtly but more like a tennis courtly, almost medieval but nothing after 1462, does she arm sweep you into a chair and give you a footrest? Opens a bag of crisps by pulling on each side? Or squishing until it busts. Does she smoke? With the boys? Girls? The popular or unpopular girls? Is she classically pretty? Does it matter? Does it matter to her? Tests? Are they short and secure, like certain poem forms? How is her prize log? In English or a tongue that few can master, and none will speak. Knows her stuff? Knows where her stuff is kept. Where is her office? Is it down a long corridor that bends and twists and soon you're in a jungle, pausing at the sound of a macaw, the chatter of the toucan, you duck under a waterfall and look out over the promontory, representing your ignorant brain. It's so big! The distant call of a jaguar terrifies you into a heart-thumping free fall. Will she share her grub in the dark cave or clasp it to her chest and you have to fight her, then and there. And remember she is strong. Does she pop quiz? Pop mints? How are her unorthodoxies? Orderly? Does she post test results like a horse race? Tests essay? Assay? Multiple choice? Does she hand you a page of choices that run down one side and up the other? Similar to a diner menu? Are they all correct, given a different cultural context? Are students invited into her house each semester? To visit her art collection. Is it comprised of the heads of former students? Or wildflowers she brought back at great personal expense and presents to each as a personalized bouquet, signifying she is expert in her field, which is us.

How to Teach

Droop. Have an unplaceable accent. Disdain information outside your country of origin. Mock directives outside your realm of knowledge. Snatch the last croissant. When someone speaks look startled, as if you had never heard anything that small produce words. If anyone tries to talk to you during the break, listen with an expression that grows more and more concerned. Scan the room for the youngest soul, one who has never been in this kind of class before; the one with a beautiful face and sensuous features, a true innocent, ripe, unsure. That one is going down.

Sit so you block the door. Insinuate you have seen combat. Never reveal it was with your ex. Write the Ten Unbreakable Rules on the blackboard with sure, strong strokes. Show no emotion when it is pointed out to you there is no blackboard. During the break go look for a bar, get stuck in a library and masturbate into the book of your rival. Return refreshed. Write down the exact opposite rules. Grab one student and use them as a shield against the others. Envision them as a frog chorus, emitting tiny beeps from far away. Cut an hour class short by an hour and a half. Use your best skills, the ones that made you famous, to identify the one student most likely to have a twenty-thousand-dollar limit on their American Express. That one is going to be a star.

Tilt back. Quote extensively from famous people, suggesting they are all in agreement with you. Have a groovy haircut. If a student is especially untalented, give them a soul shake. Sprinkle speech with colloquialisms, sexist slurs, brainteasers and bullshit. Explain long held original theories, ripped off the Greeks. Invite them to your reading, your villa, your reiki appointment, to marry you, suck your dick and paint its portrait. Give them unattainable assignments and chuckle in empathy. Become unexpectedly serious. Tell them the truth. God's honor, if they buy your book, you will get richer. Realsies. Catch sight of one, and fall for them hard; the fabulous hair, the perfect ski jump nose, the gleaming eyes, the legendary boyish grin. Oh, wait. That's a mirror.

Rise when they enter. Offer your hand. Sow questions and cultivate answers. Make them talk. Make them think. Don't let the worst preside. Fear for them. Stand up for them. Lead them not by the nose. When they get tougher, push them. When they falter, kneel. Once you were deep on the grassy path to your love. Now, you will never show others the way.

The exterminator said

we are a green company & use chrysanthemum oil not like other companies' poisons & how it works is like a queen can't do anything by herself but requires the services of these upper echelon executive ants who report a distress signal so she moves her nest & then a thousand other queens move their 10K nests because they share distress signals because they are social not like carpenter ants who meet & immediately become rivals basically like your basic high school reunion so a swarm is good & if you see more ants than possible in a frenzy over a piece of bread it's because they don't understand illness so they are trying to help the dying by bringing them food look & I said look sir I need to cancel this service immediately because I'm a Buddhist which had only become true that second & also my high school reunion sucked.

Dear Airbnb person in our basement this moment,

Mind the stack of used skateboard pieces. Each one represents a successful communication with one son on the way to the skate park. Look how many! They are perfect for your coffee cup when you can't find a coaster. If you are cold, here's a vintage coat from a girlfriend three girlfriends ago. She lived in our other son's room for six months. All we got was the coat, but still. In the mud room, you can faintly smell the dog on the rug. If your eyes sting, just let the tears flow. He was an amazing dog! Here are cookies the neighbors keep sending even though we don't eat cookies. We're not sure what hand towels are, but we have them for you. On the walls are nails from the art we threw away that had been made by my ex-father-in-law's amateur photography group. Wow was it ugly! The nails have been left to remind you that you don't have to keep that shit around anymore. Here is a booth someone tossed in a dumpster—a perfectly good booth! Thus the dharma wheel turns and turns. In the kitchen we left thyme, sugar, a stick of butter and a box of elbow pasta. Everything is an ingredient for something. Here's a quilt my grandma didn't make. She was a real piece of work. You definitely wouldn't want her ghost under the covers with you, criticizing everything you say, think or believe. In the bookcase are gift books we all gave each other to read but secretly never got around to. We offer you some games whose boards we have kicked over in rage, stormed into the street, fought off a neighbor trying to give us a cookie, got in the car and turned it on because it was so cold, pulled the damn girlfriends' coat over us, fell asleep and dreamed our ex father-in-law returned, demanding we pay his library fines (?!) then woke to find our partner beside us, drying our tears with a hand towel and showing us a badly cropped photograph of all our family, the dog in front wagging, happy for absolutely no reason, photographed for absolutely no professional reason. That's upstairs. Sorry you can't have it. But feel free to touch everything else we put here to make you feel as if this was your home.

Mister Bombastic

Lanie, Murphy and me never been to Las Vegas before. It wasn't exactly like they show in the movies, not glammy at all. Everyone dresses like shit, weaving the sidewalks, holding onto their beer neck like an unlucky goose. Traffic at a deadstill at all hours. But Lanie had some pot she snuck off her step-daughter and Murphy is proud she doesn't look forty-four. *Flirty four* as she said to the boys we'd spotted at the Denny's. As soon as she saw three of them, she's *go, go, go*. Before they leave, damnit. We followed them into the overflow lot. You guys wanna earn a hundred dollars apiece by having sex with us said Lanie in a fake hick accent. As if that would make it okay. They looked at each other. You could see they'd blown through their money first thing. Young people don't plan well. It wasn't my idea. But I didn't say no to it. Here everyone walks around dressed like a billboard, hoping to be someone's story and lol there we stood in the parking lot, about to become one. I got the shivers, had on a black glitter cold-shoulder top and it was freezing. Murphy took the skinny dude. To be expected. Lanie grabbed the tall one. Now I was at Day's Inn with Mikey from Pensacola. I don't think he had time to make anything up. I knew Lanie would be on top first thing because she'd been talking about it all morning at the pool. Murphy probably flat as a coffin, waiting to be kissed awake. She organizes her fries in a

straight line before picking one to eat. A fry line up.
Things you learn about people when you travel with
them. And here I was, next to so much youth and body
it was like a rollaway they'd added to the room. I gave
him his money right off, in case he wanted to bolt. We
sat on the edge of the bed. Shiny cheap covers. Don't
think I'm chickening out because I'm not, I said. He said
hey you want me to say you're pretty. I can. Nah, I
thought. I know what I am. You're so large, I said. Then
he smiled, misunderstanding. If he'd called me ma'am
that would have been it. Instead he wrapped me up in
those big beefsteaks. I felt all life then. Naked, he was a
monument, like on a map. I get it now, why people come
to the desert. Shock of the blooms.

Night Fishers

Water against the pier like a throat click. The churned blanket of our childhood bed. Lines curve back and fly into dark. We walked down because you wanted to see a super moon over water. On the way we pass a child struggling to keep up with his fast walking father. Father, turn to him. Your child is more than you will ever deserve to catch. We stand and watch the blank horizon. One of us is romantic. One of us is a map of capillaries. The night fishers trawl for squid. The legal limit is seven pounds. They are jigging in dark to attract the light-loving eyes. Some are successful. The rest remain hungry. No moon comes. Perhaps your charts are wrong. Below us the large, intelligent *robust clubhook*, full of ink as a pen, crosses the sea floor. I am freezing. We are rocking. We give up on the moon. As we walk away it rises behind us, huge and gold, according to timetables only roundness follows. Now the light-loving squid bite. The casters stand between buckets, feeling providential and singular, finding food where they live. A cratered moon, in waves. Thank you for catching me. Thank me for catching you.

Progeny

He was born in a caul. Lace over the body. The nurse said it was only a container. The doctor chuckled and told me Freud was born in one. Many great thinkers. Today it would be the cause of speculation, misinformation and posts. Then it was nothing. They rolled it off him without ceremony.

I would see a shadow on his forehead. I'd pretend to smooth his hair but I was brushing the past away. A strand from the amniotic sac. I often thought about the way his body appeared, as if caught in a net. Other times I wondered if it had really even happened. The doctor was long gone. The only two others in the room were him and myself and I was in a state of transit, for I had just given birth.

We lived near the sea. I can never be away from salt and spray for long. He often swam with the neighborhood children. They stood on the rocks and shouted as loud as they could, although the noise of the surf always won. He had a look to his eyes people have who are raised near water. They feel any horizon. This is the school. These are the lessons.

I dreamt of the caul. It floated above my head and when I went to touch the center, the light slid under and away like a jellyfish blot. I asked him if he ever remembered the feel of it against him but he shook his head. He guessed it was like strands that cling after you've passed cobwebs hiking in the woods. I don't know if the skin even touches it. It's not given to us to know the perimeters of our world.

He married. He had children of his own. They came out slippery, in a movement, as it is intended. Nothing clung to them. They no longer lived near the sea but they would visit. I walked with the woman he married. The sand under our feet made an impression that glittered and collapsed. He hadn't told her about the caul. She nodded, a beautiful tall woman, calm as moonlight. Whether she believed me or not I pictured him again, saw the shadows pulled back. The sack was everything, life itself, and then it was nothing, dispensed.

I'm glad I live here. The movement is constant but no light ever arrives twice. To live by water is to survive in a foreign element and a familiar one. More accurately, you are beside it. More accurately it is in view, for a while. I should know. I am a mother.

Deep Woods

We stop where the stickers stick to Sal. "Fuckin' A," says Sal, stomping. "Excuse my French, baby girl."

I'm not a baby. But that's OK. A bug buzzes my ear and then stops with a click. The sun on my hairband is heavy. Sal shows me what animals chewed. He can pick up any stick and read it like a book. He can't read a book. When I bring him my library books, he says, "Whoa, man, this is gonna make my eyes hurt." I'm not a man. I was being polite. I can read them without Sal.

But it's Okay.

Before, we were on sag chairs in the front yard.

"Nice day," says Sal.

He gets the toolbox out from under the sink but uses a bottle opener instead. He puts the band from his ankle on the fan, so it circles and slaps.

"Freedom," says Sal. "Tastes so fine, baby child. Let's go to the hardware store."

I am a child. We get in his truck. I put my hand out the window. I close my eyes and stick out my tongue. At the hardware store. Sal and me walk along the drive mowers. "Man, I could start a business if I bought that one," he says. But we never do.

We don't drive home. There's the river. It's windy and my hair blows in my mouth. Along the path Sal picks up a broken net and gives it to me. Stuff outside is free: shells, flowers, twisty wood, pieces of metal, rocks that are green.

"Man, I'd be set with a boat."

What if I was a man? That would be Okay. I feel the wind stop and it feels funny because how do you feel a thing stop? At the water's edge Sal sits, and I sit. He throws rocks. He always says the same thing when we stop and sit on the beach. A guy named Jerry told him this and then another guy ratted them out. Sometimes it's that guy's fault and sometimes another person. Sal throws out each part with the rocks.

I wait for one part. "Your mom," says Sal. "Not a goddamn other person in the whole family except my sister. That one's a princess, a queen." Sal stands up. He looks down the sand one way, and then another. No one comes in the afternoon. They come on the weekend. But there is a man throwing a stick to a dog. He stops and watches us.

"This way," says Sal. Turns, marching. I can't step in his steps. They disappear too fast. Now we're in the deep woods. Look down and keep up. I pull the hair out of my eyes because I lost my hairband.

There's a cleared part.

"Hey," says Sal, "What we got going here." I see two vampires: a girl vampire and a boy vampire. His skin is so white it looks like paint. The girl has tears in her skirt and her hair is black. They look at us and then move apart. Behind them is a very big thing they built. The girl crosses her arm with words written on it. She looks at Sal.

"Girlfriend, I'm being good," says Sal. She laughs.

"You two have fun, now." He puts his hand on my head and steers me as we walk fast down the pathway. A family has a dog and the kid has a toy car that curves around in front of us. Two people with hats and water bottles look at a map.

But was that his girlfriend?

Sal turns the truck key the wrong way two times. He leans his head on his arms and shakes. Babies cry but what Sal wants to be is a grown-ass man and that would be Okay. The seats of the truck burn my legs, but I don't say anything. We drive to the trailer and Mom is sitting in the driveway. I get out of the truck and she slams the door and runs toward us. Everyone is small. With every step I imagine I'm a baby, a child, a girl, a grown ass woman. I am a giant, stepping over the whole river and the parks and the woods, the deep wood.

Those Who Come From Circumstance

It's summer. It's twilight. Mrs. Martin is mad. She scrubs burnt bread off the bottom of the oven with a wire brush. The oven light is out; the wire brush is black, so how is she supposed to tell if she is making any progress? Outside, in the yard, Gilly faces Hank in the tent, the flashlight between them hides under his plaid sleeping bag with one, wavering red eye. It's Gilly's fourteenth birthday party. The neighbor's house is empty but the summer machines live on, sprinkler sputtering, sigh of the smoker. For the party Mrs. Martin made pizza. Gilly came in to say one girl won't eat meat. Mrs. Martin pulled off the circles of sausage. He watched her suck on a burnt finger. "C'mon Gil, no one will know." Then he says, "Hank is a vegan." Mrs. Martin pulls cheese off the pizza. That's what a pizza is, Gilly, meat and cheese. What is wrong with him? Mrs. Martin bought him a game system. She took a vacation day. She wanted to do more but Gilly didn't want, as he said, "any trouble." All he wanted was a few friends over, pizza delivered to his tent. When Mrs. Martin asks what they do for activities, Gilly is offended. He looks away. They'll watch stars. He's been sleeping in the backyard, in the tent, most of the summer. Mrs. Martin doesn't know what to think about that. She doesn't want trouble either, but then there's Hank. That boy is one step off the street. When he smiles he has a gap between his front teeth, one black tooth and eyes blue as twilight, a beautiful smile. Mrs. Martin wants to hug him, but his stink protects him, dirt, pins in his face and the slogans on his filthy parka. The girls love Hank. They ask for him. Sometimes he appears, at Gilly's house, smiling. Sometimes he's gone for days and then Mrs. Martin hears of his return, walking into the smoke and loud talk at some party, a narrowing presence, blacker, bluer. She wants Gilly to quit hanging around Hank. But words have lost their currency this fourteenth year. When she talks to Gilly, her ideas fly like rocks into a pond; all drama, noise, splash, and then complete disappearance. This summer Gilly sees adults as machines fed by corporations. They can't help but lie. Gilly loves his mother but she's one of them. Sometimes he and Hank just sit and breathe. Or they make plans to run away and be free. Gilly would go now, except for his girlfriend. She visits the tent, brings pictures of broken calves, tortured for McDonalds. Her skin smells like flowers. They stick like candy when they kiss. Hank has one girlfriend, then another. None blame him. He always leaves before they wake. Mrs. Martin pokes at the curled black bread. Now she has nothing to offer the kids. She could have ordered out, but cooking is the only thing she has left with Gilly. She made this pizza. She learned how, with Nathan, just after they were married. He unfolded the dough, brown and fragrant, pulling each corner out like a map. In the middle of making love, he used to touch her face, the route of her. At night she wakes and sees the shadow of his hand, made into a moth. They learned to make pizza in Italy, stretching the dough on the farm where they stayed after college. She thinks there's no one for her, but there is. Nathan. Earlier, listening to Gilly laugh into his cell phone, she thinks stupid to miss this, stupid to die. Nathan's needy friend sounded drunk, she thought. Why does Nathan help these people? Gilly sits in a chair, wide awake in the hospital corridor while the doctor pronounces Nathan dead on arrival. Ten years ago. Now, he sits across from Hank. "The stars have finished their lives and we're still watching them," says Gilly. "Like, they die but it takes hundreds of years for us to get the news." Hank smiles. "Old re-runs are out there," says Gilly. "They're like watching cartoons and they think it's us." Hank says maybe it is. Gilly feels in his chest, a black hole between thirteen and fourteen. The universe that throws away Hank will have to toss out Gilly too. He won't stand it. Not for all the soft skin there is to touch. The tent fills with the powerful ammonia of urine. Hank loses control when he drinks. He's been out in the streets since he was six. Inside, Mrs. Martin is on the phone speaking to the delivery person. "You won't believe this," she says, "but I need a pizza without cheese or meat." Of course, says the voice, vegan pizza. I forget, thinks Mrs. Martin, the world changes. Gilly is going to come home in handcuffs one day, after a protest. He's going to run away, to call from a train yard, to hover over oblivion like a boy on the edge, on a skateboard, willing to go over. Mrs. Martin is going to fight him, she's going to cry. She's going to ask cops for one more chance; she'll beg a teacher without shame. And somewhere in the future, as far as stars, Gilly will sit in a classroom, in the front row, raising his hand. The heavens report back, too late to dry tears, that there is someone for Mrs. Martin, beyond Nathan. She's on her way to meet him and the phone rings. Message from the dwarf star. "Hey Gil. Long time, no see, man. I'll bet you've been trying to reach me but I'm on the move, on the groove." His voice sounds cracked, tear-clogged. "I just wanted to see how you are...I know you're probably trying to reach me, so email me back sometime or call or something because I miss you and wanted to know what happened to you, peace love Hank."

The Seclusion

There aren't many examples in the family archives. We have that famous photo of Great Aunt BoDean, circa 1867, seated behind a wooden shack with ranch hands lined up on the other side, holding empty round plates. They're missing their pie, for which she was famous. Her face is hard to read in the blurry photo. We're just guessing it was a case of seclusion. I explained to my husband that's what it has always been called in the family. It's strictly female, but otherwise a cipher. No one knows when it lands, or on whom. Among my immediate kin it took my sister—odd because she was the most self-possessed, controlled person of us all. She'd been an ultra-successful business owner, wife, mother. Her flight took her across two continents and devastated them, economically. Afterwards, she regained everything and seemed completely unchanged. I told my husband all this when he asked me to marry him. He laughed it off, saying I could do what I chose. I don't think he really understood. I didn't myself. My sister and mother never talked about it. When I first rented the room in the flophouse, I planned to keep a very careful diary and finally expose the practice, for better or worse. But it's been seventeen weeks and I haven't written a thing. The longer you are in it, the more the silence grows.

Levirate

Alma attends class with her sister Eva. JJ has sisters but not like these two, same hairstyle, same dresses the color of soft foods: peach, oatmeal, applesauce. Make-up but no lipstick. They even speak in the same tones. They told JJ they're sharing a single in the conference lodge to save money. JJ knows farmers to be frugal. A seed has everything it needs. The sisters own a hazelnut farmstead east of Enterprise.

Alma is taller, Eva is smaller JJ mutters, laying out the notebooks, the glue bottles, and scissors. It's important not to mess up their names. At night, under the thick blanket of stars, gaudy and distant, he memorizes names to faces while he stands behind Big Gen, the community generator, smoking with two participants enrolled in one of the other classes. These women are younger than his students, probably in their sixties. One woman says, "I don't mean to sound insulting but it's called being a crone." "That doesn't sound insulting," JJ says. They crush their extinguished butts into a can of damp sand. "You're too young to get it," she answers. "We hold the wisdom." Hope I'd have the wisdom not to call some woman a crone, JJ thinks but says nothing. These women have paid good money to come to the community and take classes.

On the second day, when JJ unlocks the door, Alma and Eva are already sitting there. He has no idea how they get in. Eva holds the glue bottle in both hands like it was a beer, but the sisters don't drink. They've never had a cigarette. They are in bed by 8:30 they tell him, around the time JJ, who suffers from insomnia, goes to sit in the circle and listen to the interminable discussion of the members of the commune who run the conference center. One time he tried the local watering spot twenty miles away but that was bad. The circle is more open about despair. A girl with a crescent shaved onto the left side of her head wants to discuss the overuse of toilet paper. "I hope and pray y'all are composting your human waste," says a guy with a mohawk, the deep scallop of his tee shirt exposing his young, near hairless chest. "Right?" Another girl takes the talking stick. "I just came to say it's kinda wrong to bitch about guests behind Big Gen smoking big-pharma tobacco when these actual guests are the whole reason we get to be here." Finger snaps from some, frowns from others.

In class JJ walks the perimeter of the table of students, too restless to sit. On the third day after they'd returned from community lunch, someone had put two sticks wrapped with a cord to form a T in the center of the work table. "That's a Beaverwood cross," says Alma. Eva points to the indents on the surface scored by the sharp teeth of the state animal. "Yeah, that's out of concern for your mortal soul," says one of the two smokers when JJ describes the incident. "It takes seven years for the mattress to flatten back," says the other smoker, exhaling. JJ's told them he's divorced. The woman who recognizes the cross has extraordinarily blue eyes, that rare phenotype on the primate tree.

JJ stops behind a student and praises their work. "Do you enjoy being sisters?" he asks Alma and Eva. It's a stupid question but he hopes they'll relax and speak more freely. "I'm married to Thomas," says Alma, "Evie is..." She doesn't end the sentence. "We've always lived right next door." JJ imagines their men to be stern and reactionary, to have opposed this class for men who hate art and memory, though in fact he's never met them or heard them mentioned before this moment.

The class is called "Making Memory Books." JJ holds dual degrees in psychology and public health, his thesis was on the social costs of dementia. He's always liked modern art that looks old, stuff like from Joseph Cornell. In this class people are to use images from books and magazines and create a collage of their life. A woman in a colorful scarf tears her pictures, others cut them out carefully. They frown and concentrate. "How's this?" one asks. "There isn't a wrong way," JJ says. The woman in the scarf holds down the image with her thumb, pulling the other parts away in a series of small concentric eliminations. At the break they go get tea or cookies. Alma and Eva usually stay at the table their scissors closed, the cap on the glue replaced.

"Do you ladies take the morning yoga class?"

"Oh, no," Alma answers, of course. "We're both baptized. I guess they have yoga in churches now, but not ours."

"It's more spiritual than religious," JJ says.

"They bow though," says Eva. "They ring a bell. They aren't Christian."

JJ says nothing.

"It's different for you, dear," says Alma. "We understand."

Today the sisters are dressed in near matching short-sleeve shirts with contrasting vests. Under their full, longish skirts they wear sneakers.

"Those are nice kicks."

Eva shoots him a look. "I like Nikes," she says and JJ feels momentarily triumphant.

JJ carries a picture of a brain in his wallet. It's in the plastic sleeve where he used to have one of his ex-husband. He thinks the brain is beautiful, an obolid organ with a system of vessels that looks like an alphabet, literal learning curves. Most people think the brain is formed completely by adulthood but, as JJ will tell them, it's a dynamic system your whole life. The plaques and tangles that disrupt pathways in the onset of dementia have an analog in the world of forestry. That was part of JJ's thesis. He's teaching this memory class at a conference center in the woods, hoping to bring the ideas together in real life. Like everything that was once

theoretical, like his divorce, the reality is different from what he imagined. Outside sit the trees, in here sit the elders. Everything separate. Still, the class is loosening a bit, the participants talk to each other a little. Someone spilled a tea. Maybe they feel at home. JJ walks clockwise and then reverses. The sisters have finished selecting their images in a pile ready to glue. He sits down between them.
"What's the plan here?"

Alma says, "Is there scotch tape?"

JJ continually dreams of his ex who does ordinary things like washing dishes, pulling into the driveway. One time he was writing a letter which JJ couldn't quite see. In the next dream it arrived and was left on some kind of bench. He still speaks to him in his mind. He has not forgiven anything but the thoughts flow anyway without regard, like weather.

The two women who smoke with him behind Big Gen know Alma and Eva from another class. JJ asks if they're ever apart. The woman shakes her head. Eva was in love with Thomas, she says. "No," says JJ, "Alma is married to Thomas. What's he like anyway?" "He's like nothing at all, just some farmer. Tall, quiet. I only met him once." JJ asks about Eva's husband. The sky is overcast so the stars feel more distant. "Oh, Eva's a spinster," she says. "She's never been married." The other woman corrects her, "It's spinner or thornback now. Also known as a crone." JJ is ready to go home. Two more days.

JJ explains the use of the images in class on the penultimate day. He says, "What you've selected will make a biography but in feelings. Pictures help us feel what connects beneath the surface, like tree roots." He's a little bit hungover. Last night the community had a dance, wild flailing arms out on the field while a DJ played. The stars had retreated, the sky was a slate without writing. JJ walked around. An older man beckoned to him, the woman with the turquoise eyes hopped by. She held out her hands but JJ shook his head. The scene is fresh, youthful, hypnotic, but he doesn't want to touch anyone. He clasped his hands behind his back and the woman leans over to whisper into his ear. He leans down, remembering to pretend to be friendly. She whispers that the other smoker is ripping off the social security with a faked medical condition, that members of this commune are planning a revolt regarding the pot garden. JJ can hardly hear her but the words make a pleasant contrapuntal to the loudspeakers, the summer wind, the long blank night.

"It's like something out of the old testament," she whispers. "The older sister had to marry first. That's the rules. So, he marries Alma and Eva went without. Can you imagine? Right next door, all these years. It's barbaric." JJ, shocked, says he already knew. It's a lie. But he did know something. A young boy dances up to him, shaking his shoulders. A nymph, a siren, then vanished. How have the days moved so slowly and yet already they're over.

Final day, presentation day. The woman in the colorful scarf goes far over her allotted time. The man with earring cries like a child, tears he doesn't even want to control. Alma stands and picks up papers, neatly glued with pictures but shaped in a long accordion. Eva picks up the other side. The sisters stand, one story apart. They have taped their stories together against the express instructions by JJ in this class that everyone make an individual memory book.

Endless

The only places that comforted me were the thrifts. Seconds, secondhand, second thoughts. The store hours were hand-posted and usually wrong. Doors problematic, too sticky or didn't close properly. You had to push hard or pull soft.

I'd walk into them, mostly empty. Something rustling in the back. Shopkeeper parts a bead curtain and peers out. Behind them, dishes piled by the sink, an open bag of old treats. We'd both come forward to stand behind the glass case that held whatever the market had called collectible. Look down, hands hovering, not touching the glass. Jewelry for unfashionable clothes, stiff dolls, florid cards. A teapot. Tea comes efficiently in a bag now. But some still want to see leaves crumple in hot water.

Barely audible music in the background. The music is like the goods, no longer popular. But still, a powerful memory. Often there was a dog, one of those breeds with soft, short hair. A thick body of longing. The little face without answers. Pat the warm head, feel the short life pulse, unknowing.

Once I went into one while traveling. Tiny, depressed town. The shop woman stood watching me, bright eyes under severe graying bangs. Chin like a button on upholstery. She said just so you know all the romance paperbacks are on special. I hold one up. A man in a cowboy hat leans on a fence, girl in a flowered dress behind him. On the cover of another, a woman, even further back, claps her hands, while a buff hottie stands, hands to hips. Camera snaps the take, closes. They grab their things and leave.

The sale of romance novels help fund the school, she said. Four for a quarter. What kind of school needs, at most, fifteen dollars? Local high school she says. I imagine the students in crooked rows like these paperbacks. She says two will graduate for sure. In this speck of a town between wheatfields. Well, maybe two. One, definitely. I conjure her. A girl. I put her picture in the paper. The imaginary town paper. She ordered a tasseled cap and the gown was an old choir gown. Her hair is the color of a can of Pledge. Her face smooth, beautiful, bright. She won a sonnet contest while her mother fried up tinned meat and called her a waste of breath. Hard to get the count right. She uses her fingers. What will happen when she leaves her home, where she is miserable but also first.

The woman leans back, considers me. She's a judge of character. My outfit says not a romance reader. But maybe a supporter of lost causes. I go to the window and what I thought was a ceramic dog suddenly lunges at me in shrieking, furious rage. Skin back from its teeth and the roar like a siren. Jesus Christ. I twist backward, fall between the two aisles, tables of dress patterns, Disney ornaments, ice trays, plastic picks for olives and molars. Oh, don't mind him, that's just my Jack, says the woman. Seems kinda of mean, I say. My heart nearly exploded. I saw my life flash before my eyes and it was discarded objects. I loved that dog, she says. *That* dog? No, my other one. We had to put the good one down, or my husband did. I hear the shot. I mean my ex-husband. I leave with a bag of books. I'm sure they'll end up in the recycling, pulp to pulp. Sitting in the driver's seat I open a page. In the first sentence a woman's eyes flash. In the next she heavily sighs. There are no exes. Nothing dies.

Blaze

I am emptying the fireplace ashes so you can make a fire to seduce me. There's a pile of tossed bills to be burnt because they have information someone might steal. Our signatures. The pile suggests, via nonrelativistic classical mechanics, a closed system: paper made from wood, wood burning paper. No rock. Maybe a pair of scissors is lying around here somewhere. I am filling the bag as fast as possible because seductions are time-sensitive. The height, the weight, the heat, all are factors. Over the bag a cloud forms, sly and ashy, solid remnants of the once mobile. The signature of a fire. The faster I empty the ashes, the faster the ash cloud moves like that mist we drove into yesterday while we were arguing about metabolic syndrome. We were leaving the mountain and going into the valley. The mist arrived so quickly, began to rise and fall around us. We had fallen into farm country and there was a winter field, half of it rolling in dark like ground crows, the other half wearing luminous rollers like hair from the fifties. At that sight we touched hands, yours were super cold and mine were burning up. That's the difference in our metabolic syndrome. The bag is almost full. Experience proves that if I put this in the recycling bin, it will still be there in the afternoon with a stern note from the trashman. I have longed to write him back: wasn't this ash once paper and wood, items which can be recycled? Please explain.

Explain this bag full of trees transformed into a rising film. Don't just give me a pamphlet with a checkbox. I'd prefer to hold such a note, standing in the street in my negligee, from the root of the verb to neglect. I'd hope to look like someone from that Aerosmith video that would be deeply problematic today. Still we're all trying to be seduced. The sight of that field is in me and in you. Burn it up.

Epistle to the Wind

Even six months ago they would never have ventured beyond the tree line. Now we have witnesses seen them close as the hill flags. They used to cover their tracks clumsily but still they were brushed over. Now clear prints in plain sight grow by each day. Scraps no longer interest them. Previously they gobbled them down like vermin. Now they want something more. We sent runners to the pact cities for advice. We live where the road breaks down to stones, where stones have gone chalk. Every moon we wait to hear more, but all is silence. When the main council died, we had no notion what changes that would bring. The new council has been seated but no word comes for us. Yesterday there was a panic about a stolen dish. How can we tell what is a sign, what an accident. Some may be in contact with them. Some may be them. The few who have walked away have not returned. I am the last learned to write. Did it for my own pleasure since mail routes been long gone. How we may hold out is in question, but what is clear is that stones tell no stories. I put down first what I know and second what I seen. Last, what I heard from others. To any looking, I just be some woman, mad or plain stubborn, appearing to scatter snow. Pieces what I wrote down I leave here. May you collate them for the young.

Intern

The intern is an enigma. Of course, we knew that from the training. But the actual arrival is different.

I asked Abbott.
"Where does the intern sit?"
"Floating."
"The position isn't floating, it's fixed."
"That's not what Kendall says."
"Kendall is an asshole."
"Is that what you're going to tell the intern on their first day, that Kendall is an asshole?"
"It's good intel," I said. If I was an intern, I'd appreciate knowing it.

The intern came to the meeting with a pad and pen. No one knew what that was about. Maybe it only appeared to be a pen. From a hotel room. Appeared to be paper. We sent Montgomery to ask. Montgomery is the lowest link. They walked up and down the hall, talking.
I waited, around the corner.
"What did he say, Montgomery?"
"Who?"
"The intern. About the paper."
"I'm pretty sure the intern is a girl."
"What do you mean, pretty sure?"
"The intern is a girl."
"So paper, pens, is a girl thing?"

Gibiet-Nomack walked by and snorted.

Our company thrives on information. Information is better than gold or food. People followed the intern, spiritually, physically, medially. Some wanted to know if the intern was going to Burning Man.
Or I did.
"No."
"Then, where? Where is the intern going? Not that I care. But for the encrypted newsletter."
"Loma Linda."
"What the hell?"
"Largest population of Seventh-Day Adventist in the world."
I went to see Bergman.
"Montgomery isn't becoming a thing now, is he? We should never have sent him to talk to the intern."

Since the intern has no salary, I wonder how they live. I dream a dream where the intern sleeps in two ergonomic chairs. Later, I dream float past the intern, sitting on an empty stoop, eating huge spoonfuls of garbage. I wake up weeping, a thing I used to do as a child. At work I corner Abbott.
"What have you seen them eat?"
"Who eat?"
"Don't be a jerk." I tell Abbott the dream. I learned long ago that only by being completely honest can I avoid producing the shame that attracts bullies.
"Seriously? I think that intern eats very expensive vegan food most days."

"Why would food stripped of elements be more expensive when philosophies of negative capability suggests it should be less?"

"That's like asking why a muscle shirt isn't cheaper than one with sleeves."

According to office legend, this is how we two landed the Hamilton account and paved the way for the IPO.

People say they are over the intern. It's crap. No one gets over the intern. Not on my watch.

The way the intern climbs stairs. The way the intern washes a broken pair of sunglasses. The way the intern dresses in snow. The scent of the intern leaving the executive suite. How the intern has affected us. How the days before the intern wink and fade, then return in the morning, like stars.

I am in line getting coffee and when I look up from my phone, I am face to face with the intern. How many days and nights this moment brings to mind. Of course I am speechless, but it turns out the intern is not. The intern is super chatty. On and on. The line is getting held up. The intern is fatuous, inventive and quite mean-spirited. Finally, I break in. I have to do it, because only by being completely honest etc.

"Intern..."

"Oh, I'm not an intern anymore. I got hired."

I buy the intern's...former intern's...coffee. They slyly change their order to include more espresso than an

Italian revolutionary congress. At this moment a dimension in me that creates the safe space for bullies to live opens wide. Petals of the flower part. I take the first step on the thousand-fold journey.

On Trail

It gets truly vertiginous after we leave the ten-thousand-year carved gorge, ironically enough.

I'm still trailing my city irony with me.

Our turnoff is where the hills lengthen into long thighs, each with a shadowed crevice between. That's what I thought they were as a child. Crotches. I mean, give me a break, memory, I'd only myself been out of the uterus for ten years.

Past Condon, a town so small my spell check does not believe in it.

It takes us at least a day to shake off the work world. Traditionally this is marked with a fight, instigated by me. But we were running so hard from this crazy year, there isn't even time for that.

Continuing east, into wheat country. On either side of us, maize clouds and hills of lucent opal.

Even before it becomes bread, wheat beckons. A cultivated crop, sure, but it looks as if it was always here. Adam offering Eve a sheath and she says, nah, I'd prefer something hard and sweet, babe.

If you drive through yellow long enough, your eyes believe you too are rising.

We cruise along the top of the world, which is a flat globe. Over the next hill is the next hill. The undertow of clouds darken like our beloved cast iron pan. What we are running from can't exactly fit into words. It's bigger than the throat.

I read historical fiction about the Oregon trail and to be frank those words feel fake as hell. On and on about the inconvenience and everyone feeling huffy and ticked off. The lens is so our modern ills. All they need is some irony to make it complete.

As though our single thought is to clutch for safety while the products of nature mount.

Out here, the wagon tracks remain. Big sway over ruts. The sun beats us. I have miles to go. I tremble the adventure, thrill of unknowingness, even if most days I'm Alexander the Great thinking there was nothing new to discover.

The job of the world becomes clearer here. Stay alive.

There's a blue runs in all directions. The land goes to scrub and farms struggle up. What was it like to see a face come over the rise? Even now, each barn a red miracle.

The largest migration in the life of the country. If you count people. If you count some people.

In their beautiful backhanded penmanship the diaries record chaff. Outside a man sings to schoolchildren, his banjo a strumming disc. In tiers we walk past them, foot soldiers before all the land of new futures.

A Reading

No one's seen you in a while. You seem to exist on a couple of different planes. Hugging you is like trying to wedge two wrong-cut sized plywood panel together. Different women embrace you. Men who all look the same age circle you like wrestlers and then go in for the clinch. You relish both kinds of combat.

Sit, sit. The audience looks for somewhere to focus, then settles on the shiny thing, your authorized praise. The introducer is your bitterest enemy. You asked for them specifically. The list of honors secretly enumerates all your most vulnerable places. Well, not that secretly.

Now it is your turn, you up there at the podium, working the grain, rubbing out any fey frolic iamb, alert to tone deafness or floating dander; fencing the soft belly you'd pat or reconcile or denounce.

Our attention wanders. Your retrieve it. This is not your first. But you are brilliant and you have chosen this very difficult life.

All around the room, white-haired heads count ceiling tiles. Outside a red-black raven. Bird lands on the tip of a hemlock, sways confidently, although the weight differential is ridiculous. Bets are passed: raven, tree, raven, tree. A great bank of windows stands for my state. And under it a little library of books about windows.

You dedicate one to your mother. We love your mother, gently rocking in her grave. The last poem falls, we stand to applaud, or to get to you or to get away. It's not really about women. What you find sexy, dumb, and irresistible, the fount of all your inspiration, is your forever lover, death.

Then, it is over. What have we learned? That you rise, eternal. Your face when you spoke of a stranger's moment. I loved that face for a long time.

Everyone makes for the wine so wretched all innocence has been squeezed from the grapes. I have no one to talk to about this reading. People exit, legs shaky in the baked clay oven of this evening of verse. I would fly in their faces, but what good would it do. After all, as long as you rage, you live.

The last words of the reading live in my steering wheel. The smallest touch and I can make everything turn. You taught me that, after all.

Ceremony to Obliterate Failure

1. Find someone you trust. It is not necessary to know them well. But they are the one you—for some reason—trust. Print two copies of Ceremony to Obliterate Failure and read them the instructions as far as number 10.

2. Before the ceremony each of you will write down a failure, in clear language, with all the circumstances, on a piece of white paper. One page long. Print it out.

3. For example, *applied to thirteen schools and not one accepted me* or *have a one-inch stack of rejection letters, some from really crappy journals* or *we were about to move in together and then I never saw them again* but with details.

4. To the ceremony bring a clock, a beautiful piece of fabric, a lighter and a poem. Find a place with a lot of people around, but who won't really notice you. Or choose a place away from everyone. There should, however, be a wastebasket nearby.

5. Sit cross legged in front of each other. To your right, place the beautiful piece of fabric. You and the person you trust will have shopped for it together before the ceremony. On the left place the lighter. You must have

borrowed the lighter from someone who smokes too much. Center your statements on the ground between you, over your copies of the printed Ceremony to Obliterate Failure instructions and the poem. These must be perfectly centered.

6. Place your right hand on the pieces of paper opposite you and at a sign you have both agreed upon, reverse the papers, so yours is in front of the person you trust and theirs is in front of you.

7. Place the clock where you can see it. Cry. If you aren't able to cry, try to anyway. If this is yet another failure, bow. You may not cry more than five minutes.

8. Wipe your face with the beautiful fabric.

9. The one who has initiated the ceremony reads first. The one who has agreed to join in the ceremony reads second. Read clearly, without missing any part of the description of the failure. If you are in a noisy place, put your heads close together so every word is present.

10. When the page has been read out very clearly, each of you holds your page aloft and says: Do you wish to obliterate this failure?

11. Nod. Then take the lighter and burn the paper completely with these instructions. Use the other paper to scoop up the ashes and fold it into the smallest number of pieces possible. Put it anywhere on your person.

12. Wrap the clock in the fabric. Throw the lighters into the wastebasket. Hug the other person, even if you are not a hugger. Tell them that you love them. Chances are strong you will.

13. Leave that place. Avoid it for one month. After you part from the other person, call or write them immediately about how to tell the person you borrowed the lighter from that you threw it away. The other paper, just toss out. It is of minimal importance. Where it was, on your person, is an imaginary, tiny and beautiful piece of ash. Memorize the poem.

Parable of the Skatepark

I wake at my namesake. Today is the day. Gold air, baby blue clouds. Sun on the rim like a blood line across the knuckle. I feel the board falling into the empty pool, churning my hairless gut. My big feet rise from earth. I'm king of that moment, only moment that matters. I was first to wake from the pile: Doug, Mike, Cory, Whisk. They reek. Smells like cheese food, b.o and the sins of commission in here. Someone's music is still leaking out the earbuds. We planned to wake at dawn and damn here I am, the first to rise. The new park. They cut the ribbon yesterday. We're going when it opens, before toddlers and chickenhawks. The structure is clean, perfect. Swims in fog like God's own frying pan for my meat. I stake my claim. No one believes me. Cory shakes his head and glides off, red hair under his beanie makes him look like an unlit match. He peels it off, the mullet flies free. No one thinks I can do it. I been falling, failing, cracking my head like an egg. But today I'm boneless; I'm vert; 360; rise, air, land. Today, I win everything. Everyone cheers. I open my eyes. I'm in a hotel room in Spokane. The dream. I'm sixty. Don.

Night and Day

The name of the company doesn't matter now. Only that Darren and I were both in it. He had been there the bulk of his career. I was the most recent hire, hovering tentative as a joke at a stranger's dinner party. Everyone wanted me, if only for a meeting. Honestly I used it as a portal because I had always used whatever worked, whatever came to me. I was quick. I had ambitions, without a doubt. He may have had them too one time, now he was just a presence. Part of the history. He was a fixture. I was often put to the side of important matters, as female new hires tended to be. The fact that he hadn't done real work in years but was still strongly supported said everything we needed to know.

But I have a long game. Always. The future was my home. I gained something resembling power, but though he was ostensibly above me, Darren excluded himself from these modest successes. I probably would have just let him be, just left it a matter of collateral, except that wasn't an option. "He hates me, you know," I said to Thomas, my roommate. Thomas at the vanity, applying shadow in small circles, like bruises from a little hand.

"Oh, I think that's extreme."

"For him, I don't exist. I'm a phantom."

"Not hate then, is it."

People at the company weren't dumb but they were risk-adverse. They caught onto the problem between Darren and me, but either felt there was nothing to do about it or hoped if ignored it would disappear. It was some small wound to poke fun at when we gathered. A few of the women wanted to shield me; they'd been where I was. But I don't like others to fight my battles. I think that's how we weaken. We die out. He looked at me across tables, or in the circles where we sat discussing the projects, eyes dark as bullet holes. I know what those look like, it isn't a metaphor. Sometimes we'd be on teams together. The upper echelons had bigger dilemmas than Darren and me. Maybe they hoped I'd quit. Every day the contempt, the rage grew in ways large and small. A boulder ground down to a grain of sand that lodges in the eye.

At night, with a glass of wine or two, sitting on the sofa behind Thomas's vanity, I went over the latest. Thomas didn't understand company dynamics, he worked for himself. By nature a loner. He didn't even share his fantastic face but kept it for his mirror. On my peripheral, my devoted bored audience of one. Should I quit? I asked it aloud until I knew it was getting annoying. I knew I wouldn't. I had thirty years on Darren. The long game.

When I look back, I just see his face, screaming at me. It felt like the fulfilment of a promise and also as if I wasn't even present to see it fulfilled. That there were other people nearby only emphasized its relation to a dream.

For years I wondered why did I just stand there. But the fact that I did is exactly what led me to the position I occupy today. What to do in the face of conflict wasn't just a theoretical scenario to me. It was my life. To endure it, to live it whole, to feel it, withstand it, there's no substitute for that. He "retired" at the end of the year. No one asked me how I felt. They were shaken, but for themselves. Another valuable lesson. Everyone thought I never saw him again but they were wrong. I came late to pick up some pieces and he was walking out with a box. The unchanged strut of a walk; his hair had gone gray overnight. I didn't bypass him so maybe I had learned something. He said: your people. But no one heard that.

What a strange time, living with Thomas in that garbage studio that had a window facing a wall. Working for those people. Judging my performance by their criteria. I needed all these creatures to remodel myself to make a new skin. And after I didn't need them, I retired them from my mind. In the new company I was considered the "creative." They had no idea. Now my view is over other people's windows. My last job. I am over the top of it all.

Full Ride

Neddie's car died. Barfed up a rainbow of transmission fluid and flatlined. She got out and made the sign of the cross over its broke ass while a half-dozen SUV's stacked up behind her, bleating like lambs of God.

This was trouble she'd seen coming. Always been like that for Neddie. She can sense trouble, practically smell it like other people smell cinnamon buns fresh from the oven. Only one time in her life she got the signals scrambled about what was and wasn't trouble and that's how she came to birth Ronin. *They take it out of you,* said a mom from his school, and Neddie couldn't agree more. Good example: she's all day trying to set up goddamn Quickbooks, and Ro seventeen, can't find his way to finishing a single chore. Yet somehow she's supposed to drive him and his pals to the music thing. She's given him all the change from the jar and what's in her pocket now is a breath mint.

Here's what Neddie wants: a cigarette. Instead, she lifts the hood like someone is gonna stop if that lid is up. Way she looks. She left the house in Hammer pants pulled out of a garage sale free box, and an old jeans jacket Ro didn't want anymore, although he wanted it plenty at the time of purchase. No bra. Never wore one. *Why put up the wind sock in dead calm,* her ex used to say. These days she and Ro live with Gus. Today is an anniversary of sorts; twenty-four months and he hasn't hocked the computer, swung a tire iron, or skipped out on rent. Ro loathed every one of Neddie's live-in friends until Gus. Then Ro named him The One.

"I already got a name," Gus said.

"God or Mom gave you that one," Neddie says and touches her smoker's patch. Amazing the crap people these days invent to yank a total stranger back into healthful habits. "This is like a native thing, like you killed a bear." He should understand that. He is part native .

"So it's good."

"From Ro? It's a fucking miracle."

Which had not been the only one.

Neddie gives her Hammer pants a pat down and then remembers she gave Ro the cell phone too at the music event when she'd let the others out but kept Ro standing by the side of the car.

"And no smoking. I'm trying to quit and I can't take the smell."

Waving to his friends so they wait.

"Ma, more people are killed by secondhand smoke than from a single..."

"I'm not worried about secondhand smoke." She's worried about secondhand stupidity. She pushes the phone on him and barely has time to brush the top of his Mohawk, soft as a baby chick, before he gives her a smile and he's off, running across the street, with a goofy kick, hands in his pockets, jesus what a tall, handsome kid.

She scans the waiting line. Who's the band? Hard to tell from the crowd; girls dressed from every era, pairing corsets with glitter tops, skinny sky-high boots and torn denim pants. Time means nothing to these children. Time is a shopping cart. She watches two by her car, waiting to cross the street, overflowing white breasts spilling into the night, the little vampiresses. The car behind Neddie has to blast its horn to make her move, the light having gone green.

That was an hour ago; now she got no car, no cell, maybe a couple of quarters between the seats. Means she'll need to find a phone booth to call Gus as she shuts the hood. As if. Dealers have made those things extinct as a dinosaur. Communication: zero. Drugs: everything else. Yet to call someone and they actually come—that's another miracle, like when she, an atheist, once prayed to whatever misogynistic, patriarchal god might be accidentally listening. That was a dark night.

That was a night of such unclean, unleashed rain. Neddie remembers how they'd left the shelter around midnight. She could smell the trouble, saw it in how the window laid prison stripes across the face of the woman in charge. Neddie's shaking but her voice is calm. *Nah, he's just small for six.* He was four. The woman pretended to reach for a form but Neddie could tell she was going for the button to buzz 911. They call Child Services, hell itself will open. She holds him tight, leaves the suitcase. Flees.

She ran, carrying Ronin, heavy as wet sand in the downpour. She found a stairwell and squatted, lit the last of her cigarettes to stay awake. She remembers the smell; no amount of rain can scrub away street piss, its stink of derision. Sitting in a hole, with a kid, in the deluge. No ideas. None.

Out of pitch-black brick, a voice.

"That your kid?"

"I guess." Neddie gripped her knife. They weren't alone in their hidey-hole.

"Kids. They take it out of you." Ah, this is where the quote originates.

And for the first time she thought, *there will come a day when I am released.* She imagined Ro growing lighter and lighter, growing away from her. If the child took it out of you, what was he taking?

Now she's crossing the overpass. The bright day hurts her eyes a little. She forgot the sunglasses Gus urged on her until she can see the doctor. The sky is pale as a sheet of paper. She makes it out to be a sign. It's the same color as the letter Ro handed her last Monday. Letterhead on it states a college back east.

"Who helped you do this?"

"The One sat with me. I wrote it."

She read it, couple of times. Long story short, these people, these strangers have given to Ro what's known as a full ride. He's going to college and he leaves in six weeks. Tears form in her, her own tears. Really pissed off about that. She's aware of her body moving and all kinds of thoughts in her head. Can you swell with pride and contract with fear? So much shit going down the pike, where is success, what meaning to come out of the hole? What is this light?

Unthinking, she steps off the curb just as some long ass limousine comes roaring around the corner, barely making the turn. The danger veers so close she can see right into the window half rolled down, young girls in prom dresses the color of icing. Neddie balances on her toes, almost falling off the curb right into the path and there they are singing, half dozen silly geese, singing all high and pretty notes, as meaningless as a mermaid's plea.

"God, sorry!" they call, thin arms waving like octopi as the long black thing pulls away. She stands on the curb, her heart beating. What else will she see coming? A phone booth. Last one left in the city, and its right in front of her.

Acknowledgments

Bending Genres: "A Care in the World"

Cheat River Review: "Lifetime Collection"

Forklift: "Ringling"

FRiGG: "Run," "Deep Woods" and "The Intern"

Gone Lawn: "Shipping the Gods of Sitcom" and "Dream Job"

Hobart: "Arrangements"

Winner, Invisible City CFN contest: "Blaze"

Janus Literary: "Night Fishers"

Kurt Vonnegut Museum Journal: "How to Teach"

Medusa's Laugh Press: "Dear Airbnb person in our basement at this moment"

Mid-American Review: "Parable of the Skatepark"

Nerve Lantern: "Ceremony to Obliterate Failure"

New Flash Fiction: "Game Theory"

Night Train: "Those Who Come From Circumstances"

Penn Review: "Sources"

Southampton Review: "The Seclusion"

The Bureau Dispatch: "Endless"

MERRIDAWN DUCKLER is a writer from Oregon. She is the author of INTERSTATE (dancing girl press), IDIOM (*Harbor Review*), MISSPENT YOUTH (rinky dink press), and the winner of the Elizabeth Sloane Tyler Memorial Award from Woven Tale Press, judged by Ann Beattie, and the Drama prize from Arts and Letters Georgia University.